25 DAYS OF ROSES

MELLANIE CROUELL

25 DAYS OF ROSES

iUniverse books may be ordered through booksellers or by contacting:

iUniverse
1663 Liberty Drive
Bloomington, IN 47403
www.iuniverse.com
844-349-9409

ISBN: 978-1-6632-2025-7 (sc)
ISBN: 978-1-6632-2026-4 (e)

Print information available on the last page.

iUniverse rev. date: 04/27/2021

Dedicated to my Grandfather
Forest "Dick" Gatling
A Strong Man
1931-1989

CHAPTER ONE

My mother's birthday is in two weeks. Her birthday is on Mother's Day. I am so excited! I'm going to give my mother two dozen long stem red and white roses for her birthday. The roses cost one hundred dollars. I have fifteen dollars in my allowance. I need to raise eighty- five dollars to get the roses. What am I going to do? Right now, I must finish getting ready for school.

"Marcus, Marcus!" yells my mom. "Your breakfast is ready."

I put on my shoes, grabbed my book bag, and went downstairs to sit down and eat. My mother ends her phone call with Aunt Lydia. I could hear Mom asking Aunt Lydia what will Grandma cook for her birthday? I think that Aunt Lydia did not answer her because she quickly ended the call.

Mom has a special glow about her this morning. She is beautiful. She has high Chinese, Indian cheekbones with the complexion of Beyonce'. She has a shape like Jill Scott and a pearl of wisdom with words like Maya Angelou. I admire my Mom. The challenges of life have given her some blows that no one should even come back from. She gladly tells anyone that it was God who brought her through.

She interrupts my thoughts with a look that says she wants something.

I chuckle.

"What do you all have planned for my birthday?"

"Mom, I don't know. They told me that I cannot hold a secret. They aren't going to let me know anything."

She laughs with a sparkle in her eyes. Yes, baby, it is true. Are you done eating breakfast?"

"Yes."

"Marcus, grab your things so we can go."

We walk out the door and get into the car. Mom starts the car and puts it in reverse. As I am looking out the window, I think that I know where I can get the money. Grandmother can loan me forty dollars. I can pay grandma back by working off the debt.

Dad pays me ten dollars for cutting the grass and taking out the trash each week. That is fifty dollars. I still will be about thirty-five dollars short. I got this!

"Marcus, Marcus!", calls Mom. "Get off that cell phone when I am talking to you."

"Yes, ma'am."

"Baby, what are you doing on the phone?", she asks.

"Mom, I was trying to figure out what Dad, Aunt Lydia, and Grandma have planned for your birthday?"

"Baby, don't worry about that. They will not tell you if you figure it out. If they do, it will be a lie."

"Well, mother, at least I will have tried."

"Do you want your father to pick you up from school?" she asks.

"No, Mom, I will walk with Quincey to grandma's house."

"Okay, Marcus. Be safe. Text me or call me when you get to Grandma's."

"Yes, ma'am."

"We are here, says mother. "Give me a kiss, handsome."

I lean over to give her a kiss and grab my bookbag. I get out of the car smiling and leans to the right, lifts his right arm as if he was sneezing into his arm, spins and leans back dancing the dap. I could see Mom laughing while driving off.

Quincey is on the front steps of the school talking to our classmates. They walk inside the school.

"Hey, Marc. What's up?"

"Nothing," I say.

"You are the worst liar."

"Man tell me what's going on with you. I know it is about your mom's birthday party?"

"Yea, Mom wants to know what my dad, aunt, and grandmother have planned. I am short of money to get Mom's birthday gift."

"Are you going to your grandma's today after school?"

"Yea, Q, are you coming to grandma's house with me?"

"No, you are going to have to do your dirty work by yourself."

"Fine, man, be that way. I will see you after school."

Marcus walks into the classroom. "Good Morning, Ms. Kaduski," says Marcus. Ms. Kaduski replied, "Good Morning "with cheer in her voice.

"Class, Class, May I have your attention, please?" asks Ms. Kaduski. "You all know that Mother's Day is in two weeks. There is a writing contest for all of the fifth-grade classes. The topic is 'If you had fifty dollars, what would you buy for your mother?' Whoever wins will receive a free homework pass, free lunch and ice cream, and twenty dollars."

The class bursts with excitement.

"Class, calm down. For the next couple of days, I will let you work on the essay. Oh! I forgot the essay must be at least one to two pages." says Ms. Kaduski

The students get their paper and pencils out. They all begin writing with creative thoughts. I do not have a smile or a thought. I want twenty dollars. I know that there are two ways to receive twenty dollars. One, ask my grandma for the twenty dollars or two, try to earn it myself by writing the essay. I remember what my mother tells me often.

"Baby, it is not about money or gifts. It is the time and love I share with you and always remember I love you."

Just thinking about how much I love my mother and how much she means to me, the emotions became so strong. I cry. I wipe my tears. I knew from that moment what my essay was going to be about. I began writing the essay, then the bell rang, and school was over. I grab my papers and put them in the book bag. I walk towards the door. "Goodbye, Ms. Kaduski!", I say

I walk outside. Quincey is on the steps waiting for me.

"Marc, you hear about the writing contest?"

"Yea."

"What are you going to do?"

"I am going to write the essay and earn the twenty dollars myself."

"What about Grandma?" Quincey asks.

"I am not going to say anything until I know I don't have the money. Quincey, promise me you won't say anything."

"Okay," Quincey says.

We walk to Grandmother's house.

"Bye, Marc," Quincey says softly.

"Bye, man, see ya tomorrow. Text me when you get home.," I responded.

I walk in the door.

Grandma, Grandma, where are you? I ask.

"I am in the kitchen."

I walk into the kitchen. I give her a hug and a kiss.

"Hey, Marco. How are you? How was school today, baby?"

"I'm fine, Grandma. School is alright."

"Marco, you sure?", asks Grandmother. "Do you have any homework?"

"Yes. No, ma'am, "I respond. Grandma, what are you cooking?"

"I'm cooking greens, potatoes, pigtail, dumplings, a roast, and fried chicken."

I said, "I can't wait 'till dinnertime." It is days like this I wish it was the weekend. We would spend the whole weekend at Grandma. We would sit, talk, watch tv, and sing. Grandma's favorite time is sitting on the porch. She enjoys talking about how beautiful the day is, how God's creations are just that awesome. It is when she is reflecting, I get to hear something about my grandfather. ---I have never seen what he looks like. I do wonder. I've seen pictures of Grandma when she was younger. She was a beautiful plus-size woman. Grandma is what the guys would say "had it in all the right places". Grandma has dark skin, big brown eyes with high cheekbones and a smile that lights up a room and a laugh that can crack your side. Inside Grandma is as strong as an ox. She says God is her strength. Mom gets her strength from Grandma. Just when I was about to go be sneaky. The phone rang.

"Hello."

"Hey, baby. How was your day?"

"It was fine, mom."

"Please, tell your grandmother that I will be there as soon as I get off work."

"Yes, ma'am."

"Marcus, I love you."

"I love you, too, mom", I said. I hung up the telephone. My cell phone rings. It is Q. He texts me he was home. I walked into the kitchen.

"Grandma, mom said she would be over as soon she gets off work."

"Okay, baby," Grandma, replied. "Marco, is Ellis coming?'

"I don't know, Grandma," I said. "Grandma, can I help you with anything?"

"No, baby. Go rest and watch TV until everybody gets here."

"I went to the living room, got the remote, turned on the TV, and threw my cell phone on the sofa. I turned to look outside. My dad was walking in the door. I got up and jumped into his arms.

"Hey, son. Did you miss me that much? How are you?"

"I am fine, Dad," I said.

"Ellis, Ellis, is that you?" asked Grandma.

"Yes, Rella, it is me," Dad said.

Dad put me down and walked into the kitchen. He kissed Grandma.

"How is the best mother-in-law a man could have?" asked Dad.

Grandma replied, "Baby, I'm all good."

They both laughed until they cried. A few minutes later, Mom came into the house.

"Ellis and Mom, what are you two doing?", asked Mom.

"We are doing nothing. It was your Mom this time", said Ellis.

Dad said, "Nothing, Reece, just enjoying your mother."

"Ellis, you always do," Mom replied. "Hello, Ma."

"Hello, darling," said Grandma.

Grandma yelled, "Marco, it is time to eat supper."

I hurried to the table.

Grandma said, "Reece, baby, are you feeding my grandson?"

looks at her mother and said, "Marcus stays hungry just like the dog from the movie 101 Dalmatians. He never gains a pound, Ma." She turns to me and says, "Marcus go wash your hands."

I rushed to the bathroom, washed my hands, and ran back to the kitchen.

"Marcus, stop running in this house", said Dad.

I grabbed my plate. They laugh while I am putting food on my plate.

I said, "Dad, say grace over the food so I can eat," Dad says," Okay, son. Everyone bows their heads. Our father, thank you for keeping the family circle. God bless the food that we are about to receive. Let the food be nourishment to our bodies and no upset stomachs. In Jesus' name, Amen."

Everyone began to eat. After dinner, we sat in the living room talking and singing songs of praise. Then, we prayed and said goodbye to grandma. I rode home with Mom.

She said, "I miss your grandfather so much tonight."

She began to cry with guilt in her voice.

"Mother, please don't cry. You are going to make me cry", I said.

She drove the car in the yard and parked it. She turned and looked at me.

She said, "I thank God for being able to see you grow up to be this handsome eleven years old young man. My father never got to see me go to college, get married, nor his grandchild. He used to tell me that all he wanted for Lydia and me was for us to go to college and get our education. We could have a good job, house, and car. Don't worry about your mother and I. God will take care of us. Now, I have messed up the plans."

She looked at me with eyes of sweet sorrow. We got out of the car. She opened the door. We walked in the house. I started worrying but I brushed it off. I thought about the essay. I know for sure what I am going to write and that I am going to win. I began to run the water for a shower. I take off my clothes to get in the shower. When I get out of the shower, I dry off and wrap the towel around me. I walk into my bedroom. It felt strange in the sense that someone was there. I took a deep breath. I turned slowly and looked, and my dad was standing behind me.

I screamed, "Dad!"

Dad laughed.

He said, "Marcus, you and your mother are the scariest people. Look, I know your mother asked you this morning about what Grandma and I are doing for her birthday."

"Yes, she did, Dad", I replied. "Dad, were you in the house?"

"Yes, Marcus. We are giving your mother a party after church Sunday."

I asked," What else are you doing?"

Dad said, "Marcus, I'm not telling you so you can tell your Mom. I came to ask you what you are getting your mother for her birthday."

I said, "Two dozen long stem red and white roses, Dad."

"You don't have enough money."

Marcus asked, "Dad, how do you know?

"I overheard you saying you didn't have enough money. Would you like to earn the money?"

I said, "Sure."

Son, I need you to take all my weekend lawns. I have Ms. Ella, Ms. Dot, Mrs. Lou, and your grandma grass all cut by Saturday. That should make up all the money you need Marcus. Start with Mrs. Lou's yard after you get out of school. Get the lawnmower from your grandma's and ride it to Mrs. Lou. She usually keeps a container of gas for me, so I don't have to run to get gas.

"Okay, dad", I replied.

"Son, you should make sixty to eighty dollars cutting the lawns. Will that help you to get your mother's gifts?"

"Yes, Dad, I love you."

"Goodnight, Marcus, you too," Dad replied.

I put on my pj's. I got into the bed. I couldn't sleep. I tossed and turned. I looked at the clock, and it was eleven o'clock. I knew daylight was around the corner. I couldn't wait to start back writing the essay. I cleared my mind and made myself go to sleep. Now, I have Mrs. Lou's yard to cut to earn money toward Mom's gift. Morning came and the alarm went off at quarter 'til seven. I took my shower and put on my clothes. I went downstairs to eat. I ate in a hurry and rushed out the door to get to school early. As I was approaching the school, I saw Quincey.

"Quincey said, "Marc, what are you going to do about your mother's gift? How are you going to come up with the money?"

I said, "Dad gave me four lawns to cut the grass by Saturday. I am going to cut Mrs. Lou's grass after school. Do you want to come along?"

"No, not this time. Mrs. Lou likes to talk. Marc, you are going to have the money. There is nothing to be worried about", said Quincey.

"Yea, I know."

Quincey said, "Bye, Marc. See ya."

"Later", I said.

I walked into the classroom. Ms. Kaduski was standing at the door.

"Good Morning, Marcus."

"Good Morning, Ms. Kaduski", I replied.

Ms. Kaduski said, "Marcus, you are very early."

"I am here to work on my essay," I said.

Ms. Kaduski said, "Marcus, I am here if you need my help."

I said, "Thank you."

I walked to my seat and put my bag down. I pulled out the chair and sat down with a smile on my face. I pulled out my pencil and paper and began to write. The title of my essay was 'Twenty-five days of Roses.'

"I raised my hand."

"Yes, Marcus," said Ms. Kaduski.

"What does each color of a rose mean?" I asked

She said, "Marcus, your mother is blessed to have a son like you."

She began writing on the board the colors of roses:

Red – love, White – Serenity/ peace, Pink – romance, and yellow – friendship. Ms. Kaduski turned, smiled, and missed her chair. She fell as if she knew that she was going to fall. The class burst out laughing. Sheila walked over to help Ms. Kaduski.

"Ms. Kaduski said, "Thanks Sheila. You can laugh."

Sheila turned around to walk to her seat. She chuckled with her hand over her mouth so Ms. Kaduski wouldn't hear her.

"Class calm down. Let's get back working on the essay," said Ms. Kaduski.

I gathered my thoughts for the essay. I took fifty dollars divided by three dollars and fifty cents, which is how much it costs to pay for one rose. The answer was fourteen dollars and twenty-nine cents. I figured that it should be for fourteen days. I could buy a new, fresh rose. The essay: If I had fifty dollars, I would buy my mother a fresh, new yellow rose for fourteen days. I've learned the hidden truth that I have always known. Recently, this truth has caused me pain that I did not realize that it had affected me. When the truth is not dealt with properly. It hurt your family and the people you love. Love is forgiveness. Forgive begins within you. I have learned that each color of a rose stands for a different meaning. The red means love. The white means serenity or peace and yellow means friendship and forgiveness. The red and yellow roses I would give my mother every day, besides Mother's Day. My mother is my best friend. The red rose would represent how much I love her. The yellow rose represents the mother and son relationship. The pain that we will overcome. On the fourteenth day, I would give my mother the last red rose, letting her know love conquers all.

The bell rings. I grabbed my things and handed Ms. Kaduski my paper.

"Goodbye," I said.

Ms. Kaduski waves goodbye. I get outside and don't see Quincey. I walked to Grandma's with peace about the essay. I followed the instructions. I got the lawnmower and rode it to Mrs. Lou's house. When I got there, Mrs. Lou wasn't home. Thank God! Q is right. She does like to talk. I cut the grass. I was finished before six o'clock. I rode the lawnmower back to Grandma's. When I rode up, Grandma was on the porch. I put the lawnmower back in the shed and covered it up as Dad had. In the corner near the freezer, I saw this box. It was not raggedy like the other boxes Grandma had for years. This was recently new. I walked over and looked. It was a photo album and a plush throw. I had picked up the album to open it.

"Marco, Marco! I got you something to drink", yelled Grandma.

I hurried and put everything back the way it was. I walked out. Grandma was standing on the porch with a cup of cold lemonade. She hands me the cup. Thank you, Grandma.

"You welcome, baby. Marco, I am proud of you for working to earn this money for your Mom's birthday. I was waiting for you to come to me and ask like you usually do. You are growing into a man. You figure out things on your own", she said.

I smiled. I knew Grandma meant something else behind that besides me growing into being a man. It was only a matter of time.

CHAPTER TWO

I stayed at Grandma's until Dad got off work. He had a car
that must be completed before tomorrow evening. Dad is a well-
known mechanic in the area. We have people who just drop by
the house to get Dad to fix their car. Dad loves what he does so much
he doesn't mind at all. We pulled up in the driveway. Dad and I were
surprised Mom was home. Dad looked at me. Marcus this is what you
are going to tell your Mother. You helped Grandma in the yard today.
That is why you are in those dirty clothes. Dad called Grandma before
we got out of the truck. Grandma backed us up. Dad told me to cut Ms.
Ella's yard after school tomorrow. Marcus walks home with Quincey
after school tomorrow. I will pick you up from there. See if you can get
Q to help you. If he does, I have something for him too, but Marcus do
not tell him. Ms. Ella has her own lawnmower. Mrs. Lou had dropped
the money off at the shop to Dad for me. I made twenty-five dollars. I
have a week left before Mom's birthday. Dad and I walked in the door.
Mom was on the phone. She got off the phone. She walked over to Dad
and gave him a kiss. Dad titled Mom's head and whispered in her ear.

"Oh, Ellis", replied Mom.

"How is my baby? Marcus, why are you dirty and in those clothes?"
asked Mom.

"I am tired. I helped Grandma in the yard today ", I said.

I put my book bag down and walked upstairs to my bedroom. I took a shower. I put on my clothes and laid on my bed. I was so tired. I did not want anything to eat. Grandma tried to feed me. I was not hungry.

"Marcus, Marcus," called my mom, coming up the stairs. "Baby, are you feeling well?"

Marcus replied, "I am fine."

"Alright ", she said. "I am going downstairs to finish cooking dinner. I am making y'all favorite. It is with extra corn."

Mom smiled as she walked back downstairs. I was not hungry. Mom makes this stir fry that your taste buds take you somewhere else with every bite. I was starting to get sleepy. The phone rang. "What's up?"

"Nothin'. Did Mrs. Lou talk your ears off?", asked Quincey.

"Actually, she was not home. I cut the yard. I was done by six o'clock. I chilled at Grandma's until Dad picked me up."

"Cool. How much did you make today? asked Q.

"Man, I made twenty-five dollars. I need sixty more dollars to get Mom's gift."

"Wow, Marc. That is still a lot."

"I know. I cut Ms. Ella's yard tomorrow after school. Do you want to help? Ask your Mom is it ok I stay there until my Dad picks me up"

I hear Q thru the phone go ask his Mom.

"Marc, Mom said it was fine. I will show you how to pass the new level in the game."

"Cool, thanks Q", I said.

"Marcus, dinner is ready", yelled Mom.

"I have to go Q. The food is ready."

"See ya, later", replied Q.

I got off the phone. I laid it on the stand beside my bed. I walked downstairs. I went to the half bath to wash my hands. I sat down at the dinner table. Mom had made my plate. That was not the norm.

Dad looked at me smiling. We held hands while Dad said grace over the food. We ate, finished our food and talked for a while. I washed my plate, put it in the dishwasher. I kissed Mom and said thank you. I walked up upstairs, brushed my teeth. I put my clothes for school and put work clothes in my bookbag. I looked at the time. It was nine o'clock. I got in the bed and pulled the covers, set my alarm. As soon I put my head on the pillow, I was KO.

— CHAPTER THREE —

T he next morning, I was sore. I knew it was from cutting these lawns. I went to the bathroom to wash up. I brushed my teeth. I could hear Mom downstairs in the kitchen. I finished grabbing all my things. I went downstairs into the kitchen. Mom was sitting at the table like she saw a ghost. She began to cry weepingly. I put down my food, walked over to Mom. I put my arm around her and whispered in her ear "I love you mommy". She lifted her head. Mom had a look in her eye that I hadn't seen before. It almost scared me.

"I'm sorry, Dad", said Mom.

"This is Marcus. Your son", I said.

"Marcus, Marcus, Oh! Oh! I am sorry, baby. Your mother is fine. Go get breakfast, I forgot something upstairs then I will be ready to take you to school", she said.

It scared me. I've never seen my Mom like this before. I grabbed my phone. I called Dad. The phone rang so long I was about to hang up when Dad said "hello".

"Dad! I am worried!"

"Marcus, calm down. What is wrong?",asked Dad.

I came downstairs to eat breakfast. Mom was sitting at the table. She looked like she saw a ghost. She started crying like weeping. I went to put my arm around her. I told her that I loved her. She said "I am sorry, Dad". I told her this is Marcus, your son. Dad, are you there! Dad!

"Yes, Marcus. I am here. Jesus. Don't tell your mother. I am on my way home. I will take you to school", replied Dad. I heard Dad yell for Ben. Ben is the Dad's right-hand man. Whenever Dad is in a jam Ben always pulls through. I knew Dad was on his way. I fixed myself a bowl of cereal until the toaster strudel was ready. I was almost done with my cereal. Dad walks in the door.

"Are you ready to go?", asked Dad.

"No, sir. I have my toaster strudel in the oven.", I replied.

"I am going to check on your Mother. When I come down the stairs you better be ready Marcus."

"Yes, sir"

Dad walked like he was hesitating to go upstairs. At that moment I could feel the tension. I knew something was wrong. I finished my toaster strudel and apple juice. I sat at the kitchen table with my stuff ready to go. Dad was upstairs for a while. Then, I heard a car pull up. I turned to look at the door. It was Aunt Lydia. This was my clue something was really wrong. Aunt Lydia looked at me. She gave me a kiss on my forehead.

"Love you, have a good day at school", said Aunt Lydia. As soon Aunt Lydia went upstairs Dad was coming down. They both looked at each other.

"Ellis, I know. It must end. I told Mom", said Aunt Lydia.

"Truth or destruction", replied Dad.

"Truth" replied Aunt Lydia.

Dad walked downstairs. He looked at me like he wanted to tell me something. I stood up to grab my stuff. Dad gave me a hug that was almost scary. He held me for a while. At that moment I could feel Dad pain. I began to cry. It was right then Dad's tears hit my shoulder. I pulled away.

"Dad, you're crying!" This was my first time seeing Dad cry.

"Marcus, men can cry", chuckled Dad. We wiped our faces, closed the kitchen door, got in the truck. That was the most silent ride to school with Dad I ever had. When we pulled up to the school, Q was standing by the tree. I could tell he was looking for me. He saw my Dad's truck. Q began to walk towards the truck. Before I could get out of the truck. Dad softly grabbed my arm. He looked at me.

"I'm sorry, son. I am doing all I can to release this. I thought it would have ended by now. It will end! Just know I love you, Marcus", in a softly firm voice.

One tear rolled down my face. I wiped it away before Q could get to the truck. I nod my head at my Dad. "You're still picking me up from Q's house?"

"Yes, see you this afternoon", replied Dad. I closed the door. I looked at my phone. I had five minutes before the bell ranged.

"What's up Marc?", asked Q.

"I don't want to talk about it, Q. Are you going to help me with Ms. Ella yard today?"

"I will let you know after school", replied Q.

"Ok"

I rushed into class. Ms. Kaduski knew it wasn't my norm for me to come in this late. She waited until I got settled. She gave the class our instructions. She put us to work on our essay for the last part of the day. I was ready to work on it this morning. I completed my assignments throughout the day. I was so glad when Ms. Kaduski said we could work on our essay. I wanted to add something just to make it a little more special to let Mom know I forgive her. The essay read: If I had fifty dollars, I would buy my mother a fresh, new rose for fourteen days. I have learned that each color of a rose stands for a different meaning. The red means love. The white means serenity or peace and yellow means friendship and forgiveness. I would give my mother one of these roses according to our day, besides Mother's Day. My mother is my best friend. The red rose would represent how much I love her. The white rose would represent the sacrifice she has made and will make so I can have the best. The yellow rose represents the forgiveness of our relationship. In that order, I would give her the roses. On the fourteenth day, I would give my mother the last red rose. For eleven additional days, I would give Mom a yellow rose to represent the forgiveness in my heart for hiding the truth from me. Most of all, learning to forgive herself for something she did not have the power to change. Forgiveness is the power that creates love, letting her know love conquers all.

I read over the essay so many times. I thought about changing it. I knew it was from the heart. Grandma says "What does the Lord love? The truth". This essay was a truth of what a real family relationship is, that someone can relate too. Just not relate but teach someone to forgive, love past the hurt. I know I need my mother, father, aunt, and grandmother. I would love a sibling. I know that it must be some work that has to take place with Mom. The bell rang. I waited for the Mrs. Lucas' call to dismiss the walkers. This was not normal for her. I guess this is not the typical day. I waited by the tree in front of the school for Q. Q was taking longer than usual. I waited. Two of the buses had pulled off by the time he got out of the school. When Q came out of the school, he did not look like the Q from this morning. He had on sweats and t-shirts.

"Q, What's up?", I asked.

"I am going to help you, Marc", replied Q.

I was so excited. We walked to Q's house. I changed my clothes and dropped off our bookbags. While we were walking to Ms. Ella's house. We saw Toria. Toria is our classmate. Q has a crush on her. Toria, Quincey and I all grew up in the same neighborhood. When we were younger our Moms would have play dates. We started kindergarten and we were separated. We did not get to see each other. Then our parents got busy with the demands of life. We did not get to see each other. Q began to start fidgeting as Toria was walking towards us.

"Hey Marcus and Quincey", said Toria.

"What's up?" replied Marcus.

"Hey, T", nervously replied Q.

"I haven't seen y'all in a minute. How are you?"

"We are good, Toria. We miss you too", replied Marcus.

"Quincey, What is wrong with you? You usually talking", said Toria.

Toria was looking nice today. "T, you look nice today."

"Thank you, Marcus". Toria smiled with a look in her eye.

"You look extra nice today. That's why I can't talk. My eyes are on you", smoothly replied Q.

Toria stopped and looked, like she couldn't believe what came out of Quincey's mouth. She was so shocked.

"Thank you, Q. Where are you headed?"

"We are on our way to Ms. Ella's house" replied Marcus.

"Oh ok. I just passed by she is sitting on the porch"

"Thanks, T. Good to see you"

"You too Marcus. Lay ta, Q", replied Toria. She walked away. Q was staring like he couldn't believe. Man, what was up with that?

"I don't know. Marc, I like that girl so bad. I become stupid", answered Q. We laughed. Ms. Ella was on her porch just as Toria said. Ms. Ella was rocking away in her rocking chair. When we walked up on the steps to the porch. Ms. Ella yelled, "Oh My God! Sweet baby Jesus! John!"

Ms. Ella turned pale as a ghost.

"Ms. Ella, this is Marcus. This is Ms. Rella's grandson" said Quincey.

"Oh Jesus! Ok. I will call Rella", replied Ms. Ella.

"I am here to cut your grass, Ms. Ella", said Marcus.

"Ok, baby. The lawn mower in the back in the shed"

We walked around the back of the house to the shed. We open the shed. Quincey helped me to move everything from around the lawn mower to get it out. While I was preparing to get the mower started. Quincey was picking up the limbs out of the yard. We finished before six –thirty. We cleaned up, put the lawn mower back in the shed, and walked back to Q's house. Q took a shower first, then me. I put my school clothes back on so Mom wouldn't have a clue. Dad picked me a little after seven. I had texted Dad earlier to let him know Quincey helped with picking up the limbs in the yard and cutting the grass. Dad came in and gave him twenty dollars for helping today. When I got in the car. Dad said Ms. Ella paid us fifty dollars. I made fifty dollars. I was so excited. I have seventy-five dollars. I only need twenty-five dollars to get Mom's gift. I have Ms. Dot yard tomorrow. I know Grandma took us over there. It will give her time to sit and talk with Ms. Dot. What will the truth reveal?

— CHAPTER FOUR —

I didn't want to get up that morning. I was sore and tired. I understood what Dad was saying about cutting these yards. He would come in nine or ten at night. I hit the snooze so many times. I didn't realize it was that late. I threw on some clothes and my work clothes in my bookbag. I went to the bathroom and brushed my teeth and my hair. I raced downstairs. I heard Dad yell Marcus! I knew what that meant. I grabbed my phone from the basket. On certain nights of the week. Mom and Dad made me put my cell phone in the basket. It is to give us a break from our cell phones. Just in case we have family time we can. The last few days Mom hasn't left their room except Aunt Lydia taking her to the doctor. I am scared to see her because I know I look like the reminder of her pain. Again, it was another morning Dad and I rode to school in silence.

"Marcus, go to your grandma after school. She will take you to Ms. Dot. Same thing applies to Quincey. If he helps, I will pay him. If he doesn't no pay, I will see you when I get home from work.

"Hello."
"What's up, Marc?' asked Quincey.
"Nothing. I have to get to class."
"Marc, something going on. Your Dad has dropped you off to school almost every morning this week and is picking you up in the evenings. Something is up? What's going on with Mrs. Reece?", asked Q.

For the first time I really cried. That moment I felt like I was the blame why Mom couldn't come out of her room. It hurt me! It hurts that Mom is hurting that bad. It is nothing I can do. I don't even know what my grandfather looks like. I hear from other people say I look like my grandfather. Imagine how that makes me feel. Q put his arm around me. He never saw this side of me before. He helped me into the school. He got me to the school counselor Mr. Davion. Mr. Davion is hard core. He is a military veteran of the Air Force. He helps out with the JROTC classes at the high school sometimes. He was about to leave for a class when Q brought me in his office.

"Good Morning Mr. Davion. It's Marcus. I don't know what's wrong? I think it is about his Mom. I asked asked him, he starts crying so hard. He will not stop crying."

"Quincey, I got him. I will call Ms. Kaduski. Wait, I will write you a pass to class."

Mr. Davion handed me the pass. As Q was walking out the door. He was on the phone calling Ms. Kaduski class. I was worried. I never saw Marc like this before. He was still crying once I left the office. I couldn't focus in class until I knew Marcus was ok.

Mr. Davion sits besides Marcus. He does a breathing technique. Marcus you had an anxiety attack. You need to go home. I am going to call your Dad.

"No!" yell Marcus.

"Marcus, what is it?", asked Mr. Davion.

"Call my grandma. I don't want to talk about it."

"Marcus, you need to talk about it.", said Mr. Davion.

"Please, call grandma", said Marcus.

"Ok. Marcus"

Mr. Davion calls Marcus' grandmother. As Mr. Davion dials he is watching me as if he is studying me. Grandma picked up the phone.

"Hello"

"Hello. Ms. Rella. This is Mr. Davion the school counselor. I have Marcus in my office. He had an anxiety attack. He needs to be picked up from school."

"Anxiety attack. Oh my God! I am on my way.", replied Grandma.

Grandma got dressed and put on her favorite shoes. She drove to the shop to see Ellis. Dad knew when he saw Grandma drive up at the shop something was wrong.

"Rella!"

"Ellis, calm down. It is Marcus."

He puts his head down. He walks to Rella's car.

"What happened?", he asked.

"Marcus had an anxiety attack."

Rella we have to do something now. It is affecting my son. It is affecting me. My son knows he looks like John."

"You are right, Ellis. Have you tried talking to Reece?", asked Rella.

"Yes, she just goes into a deeper depression."

"Jesus! Let me go get Marcus. I make sure he rests before going to Dot's house."

"Thank you, Rella. Let me know if you think he isn't up to cutting the grass. I will call you later."

Grandma picked me up from school. Mr. Davion spoke with Grandma. I don't know if she told him. He looked at me through the window with tears in his eyes. I knew it was serious. Grandma opened the door. She signed the book to check me out. We walked out of the school to the car. Grandma took her key out to open the car door. She gave me the biggest hug. The tears begin to roll down my face again. I cried softly all the way back to Grandma house. I got on the sofa. Grandma wouldn't let me go to my room. I cried till I fell asleep.

CHAPTER FIVE

When I woke up, I could hear Dad's voice. He was talking to Grandma. I could hear Dad saying he did not know how much more he could take. I know what happened to me did not help. He is really worried. What can I do to make him feel better?

I got up off the sofa. I look at my phone for the time. It read 2:45 p.m. I knew Quincey would be out of school soon. I know he is heading right over to grandma's house. Just when I was about to put on my shoes, I heard Dad walking out of the kitchen. I looked up. Dad is walking into the living room. He sat on the sofa beside me. He leaned over and gave me a hug. I felt tears dropping on the top of my head.

"Dad are you crying?", I asked.

He chuckled. "Marcus, yes it does not make you weak for being a man. I love you, son. I am sorry that you have to go through this. I am working hard to solve this problem. It is unfair to you. You deserve to have a childhood to some degree. You have to deal with this from birth. I thought it would be better by now. I take some of the blame because I should have taken control of the situation before you came into the picture Marcus. I am going to fix this.

At that moment we hear a knock at the door, Grandma opened the door.

"Hey Q! How was your day?", asked Grandma.

"Hello Ms. Rella. My day was good. How's Marc?", he asked.

"Come see for yourself.", said Grandma.

Quincey walked slowly around the corner of the door. He saw me sitting beside Dad. He almost leaped across Dad to hug me.

"I am sorry Mr. Ellis. I am just glad Marc is ok. I had never seen my friend that way before. It scared me.", said Q.

"Q, it scared us too!", said Grandma.

"Well, let's get to work. We have Ms. Dot grass to cut today.", said Marcus.

"Marcus, you need to rest. I will take care of that yard.", said Dad.

"No! Mom's birthday is less than five days away. I want to see her smile. Let's make her smile, Dad.", said Marcus.

"Ok, Son.", replied Dad.

"Well, let's go to Dot's!", said Grandma.

Grandma took us to her best friend's house. Her name is Ms. Dorothy Nokes. We call her Aunt Dot. We got out of the car.

Aunt Dot yelled, "Hey Rel'."

We walk in, and Aunt Dot is sitting in a La-Z-Boy recliner, flipping the channels like a coin. She puts the remote down, stands up and gives Grandma a hug.

Aunt Dot said, "Rel', Marco is looking more like John every time I see him."

"I know," said Grandma.

"How is Reece dealing with this?"

"Not too well," Grandma replied.

Quincey and I gave Aunt Dot a hug. She told us where the gas was for the lawn mower and gave us the key to the shed. We took the key to open the shed. For the first time, I didn't need help to get the lawn mower out of the shed. Q started picking up the tree limbs and the other debris out of the yard. It did not take us long to do Aunt Dot's yard. Grandma and Aunt Dot were on the porch. We walked up the ramp. Aunt Dot pulled me towards her. She whispered in our ears to go into the kitchen, to eat the ice cream, Capri Suns, and candy. She said if it's gone, then Dalton had eaten it all. Dalton is her grandson. We found two Capri Suns, one ice cream sandwich, we shared. After Quincey and I finished eating, we went outside to play. We played for hours. About eight o'clock, Grandma walked out the door.

"Boys, time to go home." We ran to get into the car. Quincey and I waved at Aunt Dot.

Aunt Dot yelled, "Bye, Rel'! See ya tomorrow!"

Quincey and I fell asleep in the car. Grandma dropped Q at his house and Quincey's mother said, "Rella, thank you for dropping Quincey home. You're always spoiling these boys."

Rella said, "Liv, I do it now while I am here on this earth. I love the boys very much. They stay out of trouble. Quincey is an Honor Roll student. Liv, be very proud, because you could be sitting in juvenile court or somewhere."

Olivia smiled and said, "Thank God for you. I am blessed. Have a good night, Ms. Rella."

Grandma replied, "You too, baby."

She drove off.

When we got home, she said, "Marco, go take your shower and get ready for bed."

"Yes, ma'am." I got out of the car and Grandma walked in with me. When I walked through the door. I heard Dad talking. We walked through the kitchen. In the living room was Mom sitting up watching TV. I ran, gave her the biggest hug.

"I love you, Mom!!", said Marcus.

Grandma and Dad both smiled and hugged. They look at each other and say "God answers prayer".

CHAPTER SIX

I went back to school the next day. Ms. Kaduski was so glad to see me. "Marcus are you feeling better?", she asked.

"Yes, ma'am.", I replied. I put my books away. She had all the agenda on the board. I saw she said today was the last day to change anything on our essay for Mother's Day. I did all my work. It seemed like the math assignment wanted to give me the most trouble today. Especially when I wanted to see if I needed to change anything in the essay. I finally finished the math right after lunch. The class came in from the bathroom. I waited for Ms. Kaduski to get settled before I asked for my essay. While I wait, I pull out a book that I have been reading "This Is Where It Ends" by Marieke Nijkamp. This book is a realistic, sadness of what we don't know what we are going to encounter each time we enter this school. I finished reading chapter five. I put my book mark in the book. I closed the book and put it on my desk. I walked to Ms. Kaduski's desk. "Ms. Kaduski, may I have my essay, please."

"Yes, Marcus", she replied.

I looked over the essay. I changed it. This time it fit what my heart wanted to say. At the end of the day, I walked out of that classroom with an assurance that if I don't win. I knew I had put my heart into this essay. When the bell rang, I waited for Quincey by the trees. Q wasn't slow meeting me that day. We both were happy we didn't have to cut no one yard that day. We both walked home wondering who was going to win this essay contest. Then it was silence as we continued to walk home. I could tell Q was looking at me. You can feel that someone is looking at you. I knew Q wanted to ask or know the truth about why I had my anxiety attack. I waited until we reached Grandma's house. I sat on the front steps of the porch. Q sat beside me. Q, I know you want to know what happened to me the other day. You remember in the movie "Harry Potter", Harry was the family secret and his family mistreats him.

"Yes, what about it?", asked Q.

"Well, I knew I looked like my grandfather. I never saw pictures of him. When my mom was a little girl he was killed a few days before her birthday. She goes into a state of depression a week before her birthday. Most of the time it will last a few days and go away. This time she completely shut down. She called me by my grandfather's name. Mom doesn't want to discuss it. I think she is refusing to get help. Dad is getting tired of the situation making me feel like this. He has constantly reminded me. I am not a mistake. You haven't done anything wrong. This is something that happened before I was thought about. My mom just needs to forgive herself, get therapy, because I need her. This has put a strain on our relationship. I feel like I am the blame for everything. I know I'm not, but this doesn't help. This is what the pastor is preaching about life situations that you can't control. You do what is right and go with the flow."

Q chuckled. "Yea, Miss Rella slogan "what do God loves......... the truth." Marc you know your truth. This will make you stronger. All these years we have been best friends, you never shared that with me. This let me know how strong you are. I love you, man. I need you! I need your Dad too. You are the example of what a father and son relationship should be. My secret is that your Dad has gotten up early Saturday mornings, came to my house, woke me up, that I can learn how to fix things around the house for my mom. He has shown me how to cut grass. Your grandma has come by the house to show my mom how to cook. If she is sick, your grandma will take care of her. Your grandma and your dad are a team that works secretly."

"Thanks for letting me know this Q. I wonder who else grandma and dad is helping in the community. I wonder why grandma couldn't help mom or mom wouldn't allow her to help?"

"It isn't for you to understand. Marc, let me get home before mom is calling."

"Ok. Text when you get home, Q. We hugged. While Q walked away for the first time. I wanted to say come back. I need you. I think he knew after our talk. We need each other so much more."

CHAPTER SEVEN

Dad picked me up from grandma's house that night. Mom finally told her job about her depression. She has cut back her hours at work. Ben has been helping Dad so much at the shop. They received a new contract with a marina and limo service. This means more money coming in for the family. I noticed Dad hasn't had the chance to cut the grass. Yea, this is my day off from school. I am doing what a good man would do. I washed up, changed into my sweatpants and t-shirt.

Quincey said, "You are serious about getting this money. I'll holla atcha tomorrow. OH! Did you turn your essay in today?"
"Yes, I turned it in today," I said.
"Okay, Marc. Later," Quincey said.
"Bye," I replied.
Marcus walked into the kitchen.
"Mom, I am going to cut the grass."
"Alright, baby. Be careful. I will call you when dinner is ready," said Mother.
I went into the backyard. I pulled the lawn mower out of the shack. I poured gas into the mower. I began to cut the grass. It took about an hour for me to cut the front yard. As I turned to take the mower back to the shed. I saw a sheet covering something in the corner of the shed.

When I was about to walk over to see what it was. Dad drove up in the yard.

He said, "Hey, son! Thank you for cutting the grass."

He opened his wallet and gave me twenty dollars. Mother opened the door.

She said, "Hey, Honey. Dinner is ready."

Dad and I rushed into the house to wash our hands. We ran to the table smiling, knowing Mom was going to fuss.

She turned around, saying, "You two need to stop this before one of you gets hurt."

She sat down to eat.

Dad said, "Good Lord, Good eat, Let's break our tanks and eat. Amen."

We all laughed. After we all ate, I helped my Mom with the dishes.

She said, "Thank you, Marcus."

"You're welcome."

"Goodnight," Mom said. I took a shower and got into bed. The next morning, I woke up and started to get ready for school. I went downstairs to fix breakfast. I got a big bowl and cereal from the cupboard and the milk from the fridge. I sat down to eat the cereal. As I am sitting there, I think about the essay and the twenty dollars that my father gave me. I wanted to earn money for Mom's birthday gift. I finished breakfast and walked to school. I got there, and Quincey was excited.

"Are you ready to find out who won the contest?"

I replied, "NO. I have the ten dollars."

Quincey said, "Marc, you can take the money and buy something."

"Yea, Q," I said. "See ya later." I walk to class.

Ms. Kaduski says, "Marcus, I am very proud of you."

I said, "Thank you."

"I walked to my desk. The announcements came over the intercom.

"Boys and Girls! The winner for the writing contest is a tie."

"Quiet, Please. The winners are Marcus Bishop, and Latoya Chi. Would the winners come to the office, please?"

Ms. Kaduski's eyes were full of tears and her heart was filled with joy. I got to the office.

The principal, Mr. Alphabeto, said, "Congratulations! Since, there was a tie, we are going to split the twenty dollars."

I smiled with relief.

I shook Mr. Alphabeto's hand and said, "Thank you."

I walked back to class. Ms. Kaduski had a party prepared for me. The bell rang and I walked to the store to get the roses.

Ms. Lovely said, "Hello, Marcus. Are you here for the roses?"

"Yes, ma'am, I am here for the roses," I replied.

Ms. Lovely went to get the roses. While I waited; I found my mother a beautiful card.

The card said: "A Mother like you deserves a rose."

I read the card. I knew it was perfect. Ms. Lovely handed me the roses.

I said, "I would like this card also."

Ms. Lovely rang me up on the register.

"Your total is forty-three dollars and sixty-one cents."

I gave her forty-five dollars. My change was one dollar and thirty-nine cents.

"Thank you, Marcus," said Ms. Lovely.

I walked to my grandma's house, to hide the roses and card. I knocked on the door. Grandmother (Rella) answers the door.

"Marco, what's going on?" she asked.

I asked, "Can I hide the roses and card here?"

"Yes, baby. Are you coming in?" asked Grandma.

"No, ma'am. See you later, Grandma," I said.

I walk home thinking how much my mother is going to love the roses. When I got home my dad was hiding a big box in the shack. I waited until he finished hiding the box. I came around the corner slowly to try to scare my dad.

My dad turned around and said, "Marcus, you can't scare me."

"Dad, you are so unfair sometimes," I replied.

Dad rubbed my head and laughed. I asked, "Where is mother?"

Dad replied, "She is with Aunt Lydia doing women things."

We both laughed as if we were glad that we were men.

Dad said, "Well, it is going to be the men tonight."

I said, "Yea, I'm glad."

In the back of my mind, I was thinking that it was going to be hard to find out what was in the box. I enjoyed the time I spent with my father.

Early Saturday morning, I snuck out of the house to the shed to see what was in the box. I opened the box; it was a painting of Grandfather, Mother, and Aunt Lydia as little girls. I put the painting back in the box. I ran back into the house and upstairs to the bed. I got into the bed just in time, because Dad had awakened. I pretended that I was asleep. Dad walked into the bedroom to check to see if I was okay. He walked out, closed the door. Next, he took a shower. He put on his clothes, got into the car and left. Next, I heard Grandma humming "Jesus is the Best Thing that Ever Happened to Me." She walks into the bathroom to wash her hands. She starts cooking. I smelt bacon, sausages, pancakes, and eggs. I knew Grandma was going to call me soon. I got up and took my shower. I put on my clothes, went downstairs, and played my PlayStation 4. I heard a knock at the door.

Quincey yells, "Marc, open the door."

My grandma opened the door.

She said, "Quincey, don't you do that again. Marcus is asleep."

Grandma, I am right here, I said.

Grandma said, "Come in and sit down. Quincey, honey, I'm sorry. Marco didn't let me know he was up. Would you like breakfast?"

"Yes, ma'am."

Quincey and I went into the living room to play the PlayStation 4.

Grandma yelled, "Breakfast is ready! Go wash your hands!"

Quincey and I rushed to the bathroom and to the table. I was about to sit down. Quincey moved the chair from under me. I fell to the floor in slow motion on my butt.

Grandma asked, "Honey, are you okay?"

"Yes, ma' am."

Grandma walked over to Quincey to hand him his plate. I saw her left hand come up and smack Quincey upside his head.

She said, "I know you were playing, but it was also dangerous.

She walked away with a look of sternness. After breakfast, Grandma took Quincey and me to Dave and Buster, shopping, and visiting.

I got out of the shower. I put on my clothes and went to bed. I heard Dad walk in the house.

Grandma asked, "Ellis, have you heard from Reece?"

"No, Lydia did call me and said that Reece is doing fine. She was talking about John and how Marcus is growing into the looks of John.

Rella asked, "What is Lydia doing about Reece?"

"She is trying to keep her mind off of it." Dad replied.

"Rella, why does Reece act this way? She always talked about how he wanted the best for her and Lydia. How did John die?"

Grandma starts to cry.

She said, "The truth will set you free. Ellis, the picture I gave to you to use for the painting is the day John died."

Dad said, "What, Rel'? You saying?"

"Yes, Ellis," said Grandma. "John's birthday was May 8th."

"Reece, Lydia, nor you told me that."

"I know, because of Reece."

"What happened?" Dad asked.

"This is before we moved to North Carolina. It was the Saturday before Mother's Day. John had just come back from the store. He brought the girls a ball. He yelled for them to come outside. They came rushing to the backyard. They were rolling and kicking the ball. Reece kicked the ball; it rolled into the neighbor's yard. He was prejudiced. Reece went to get the ball out of the yard. John saw the top of the shotgun in the window. He yelled 'Reece, run!' Reece wasn't understanding and continued to get the ball. John ran and grabbed Reece just in time. It was too late for John. He was shot in the back and neck. Reece fell to the ground when she heard shots. John's body fell directly on top of her. She was covered in blood. After that day, Reece was in a mental center for at least two years. She continued therapy to forgive herself. We moved from Colvation, South Carolina to Bates, North Carolina. We got to North Carolina and Reece started talking. She never stopped. I tried to get her to talk about her father, but she would say "I miss Daddy. It was my fault." She would say what he wanted for her and Lydia. Today makes fifty years John has been dead. Tomorrow is Reece's fortieth birthday."

Dad said, "I see. You were hoping the painting of that picture would help her remember and will help Reece to stop blaming herself for his death."

"Yes, Ellis. It has been too long." she said. "Reece feels that Marcus looking just like John is her way of being punished."

Dad and Grandma embrace. They both realized that it was eight o'clock.

Grandma said, "Marcus, Marcus. Wake up!"

"Good Morning, Grandma," I said.

I took my shower. While I was taking my shower, I thought about what I overheard. I knew that I had to prove my love Mom. I want Mom to know I wasn't her punishment. I was reminded that Granddad loved her so much.

"I will read my essay in church."

I rushed to get ready for church. Grandma saw that I was on edge.

"Marcus, anything wrong, baby?" she asked.

"No, Grandma," I said.

Dad yelled for Grandma and me to meet him in the car. When we got to church, I went on the search to find Mother Hamm. Mother Hamm did the announcements in church. She was seventy-five, a widow, a mother of five children, and a grandmother of eight. Mother Hamm is "fas'." That is what Grandma called it. I found Mother Hamm flirting with Deacon Roye in the pastor's study. I was getting sick looking at them. I walked right between them.

I said, "Excuse me."

Mother Hamm looked, leaned over and whispered in my ear.

She said, "If you ever do that again, I am going to hit you so hard that you are going to think you were in the upper room with Peter. Now, what the hell do you want?" she said.

First, you are in church, cursing is wrong. Second, do I need to tell my Grandma?"

She reluctantly said no.

"Thank you," I said.

"I want to read my essay I wrote for the writing contest at school for my mom."

Mother Hamm said, "Yes, baby. I will call you after all the announcements."

"Thank you, Mother Hamm," I said.

I walked back into church. I sat with mother and Aunt Lydia. Pastor Allen called for the announcements. Mother Hamm walks to the podium.

"People of God, these are the following announcements: June 3rd, Pastor Allen and congregation will be at Deliverance Temple; June 8th-12th, Pastor Allen will be in revival at Praise and Worship Center; June 20th, Minster Lanell Manthen will be ministering at Joy Ministries."

She winked her eye at me. I walked to the front of the church.

I said, "Happy Mother's Day to all the mothers. I wrote this essay for my mom, entitled Fourteen Days of Roses."

If I had fifty dollars, I would buy my mother a fresh, new yellow rose for fourteen days. I've learned a hidden truth that I have always known. Recently, this truth has caused me pain that I did not realize that it had affected me. When truth is not dealt with properly. It hurt your family and the people you love. Love is forgiveness. Forgive begins within you. I have learned that each color of a rose stands for a different meaning. The red means love. The white means serenity or peace and yellow means friendship and forgiveness. The red and yellow roses I would give my mother every day, besides Mother's Day. My mother is my best friend. The red rose would represent how much I love her. The yellow rose represents the mother and son relationship. The pain that we will overcome. On the fourteenth day, I would give my mother the last red rose, letting her know love conquers all.

After reading the essay, I walked back to my seat.
My mother cried and hugged me and said, "I love you."
Aunt Lydia looks at me and says "Thank you. You did a good job."

After service, Pastor Allen gave me twenty dollars.
"Thank you, sir."
Pastor Allen said, "shhh! Our secret."

Everybody arrived at our house. Dad opened the door for mother. Everyone screamed, "Surprise!"

Mother smiled and thanked Dad, Grandma, and Aunt Lydia. Mom socialized with friends and family. Grandma called everyone's attention for cutting the cake and gifts. Mom cut the cake. Grandma started passing out gifts. Dad, Grandma and Aunt Lydia's gift was last. It was the box I saw in the shed. My mother opened the box with excitement. She saw the painting of Granddaddy, Aunt Lydia and herself.

She started crying and said, "Please, forgive me."

Aunt Dot said, "Reece, baby, it was never your fault. God gave you the opportunity to see your Father every day. Marcus is a living reminder of how much your Father loved you and Lydia. This is not your punishment. This is a joy. The relationship you and Marcus have continues to build on it."

Mother hugged me very tight. She asked me to forgive her.

"I did not have any hard feelings towards Mom. Mom didn't show any hard feeling towards me. I apologize for my hidden intentions in my heart towards you. I know I told you, I love you, Marcus, and I do. Let's begin a new relationship today."

I walked in the kitchen, took a rose out of the vase. I walked through the crowd. I tapped my mom on the shoulder. This red rose represents our love. This is the beginning of your fourteen days of roses and a new relationship.

"Marcus, thank you. Give me a hug," she said.

This is what forgiveness is all about. Mom stands up. She says "Excuse me! May I have everyone's attention, please. During all this sadness, confusion, God has brought us joy". She screams "We are pregnant!" Everyone excited begins to congratulate Mom, Dad and me.

I am going to be a big brother. This is a true new beginning.

Printed in the United States
by Baker & Taylor Publisher Services